Children are workers, too.
Many children are helper workers.
Are you a helper?

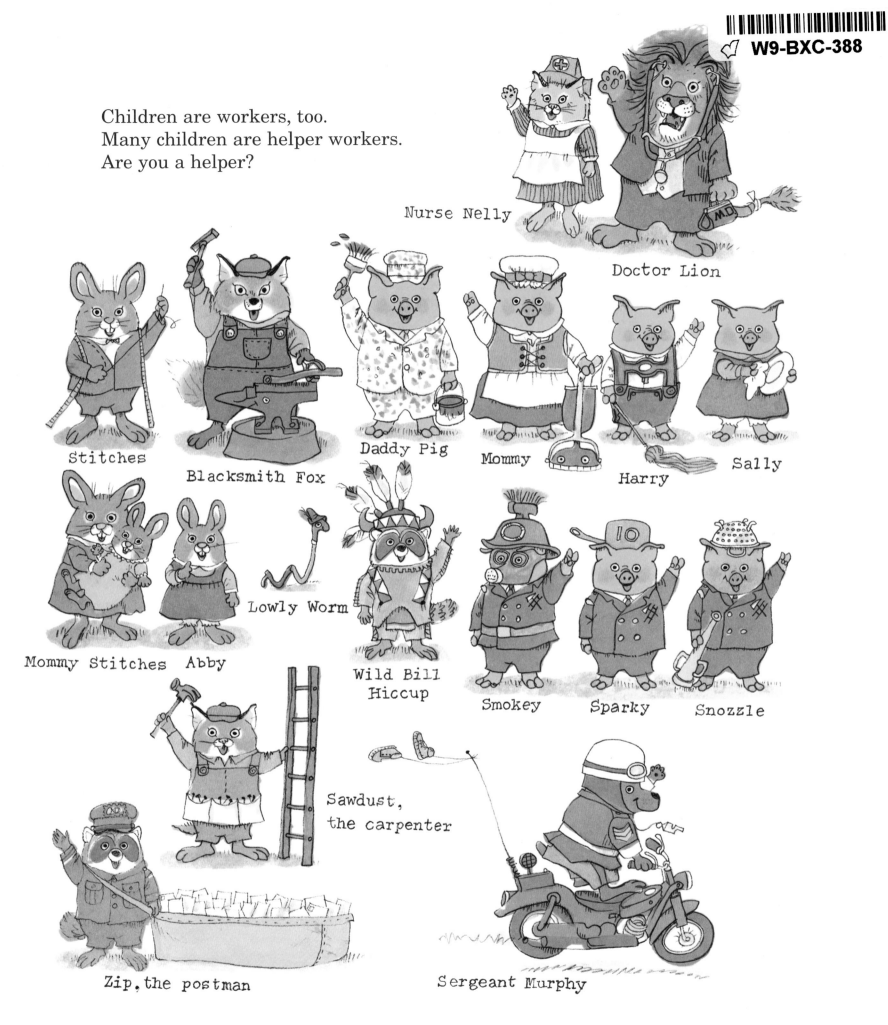

Nurse Nelly

Doctor Lion

Stitches

Blacksmith Fox

Daddy Pig

Mommy

Harry

Sally

Mommy Stitches   Abby

Lowly Worm

Wild Bill
Hiccup

Smokey

Sparky

Snozzle

Sawdust,
the carpenter

Zip, the postman

Sergeant Murphy

Come! Let us see the many
different workers working at their jobs.

A GOLDEN BOOK • NEW YORK

Richard Scarry's
WHAT DO PEOPLE DO ALL DAY?

This is Busytown.
My, what a nice town!

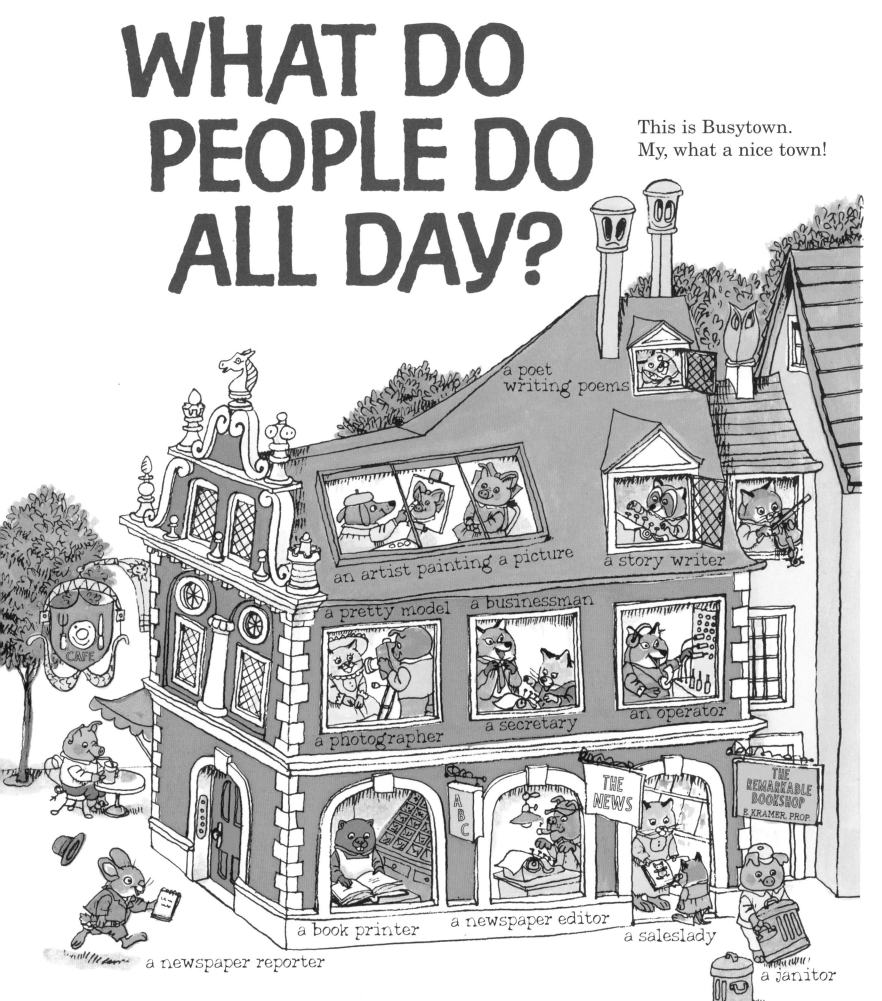

a poet writing poems

an artist painting a picture

a story writer

a pretty model

a businessman

a photographer

a secretary

an operator

CAFE

THE NEWS

THE REMARKABLE BOOKSHOP
E. KRAMER, PROP.

ABC

a book printer

a newspaper editor

a saleslady

a newspaper reporter

a janitor

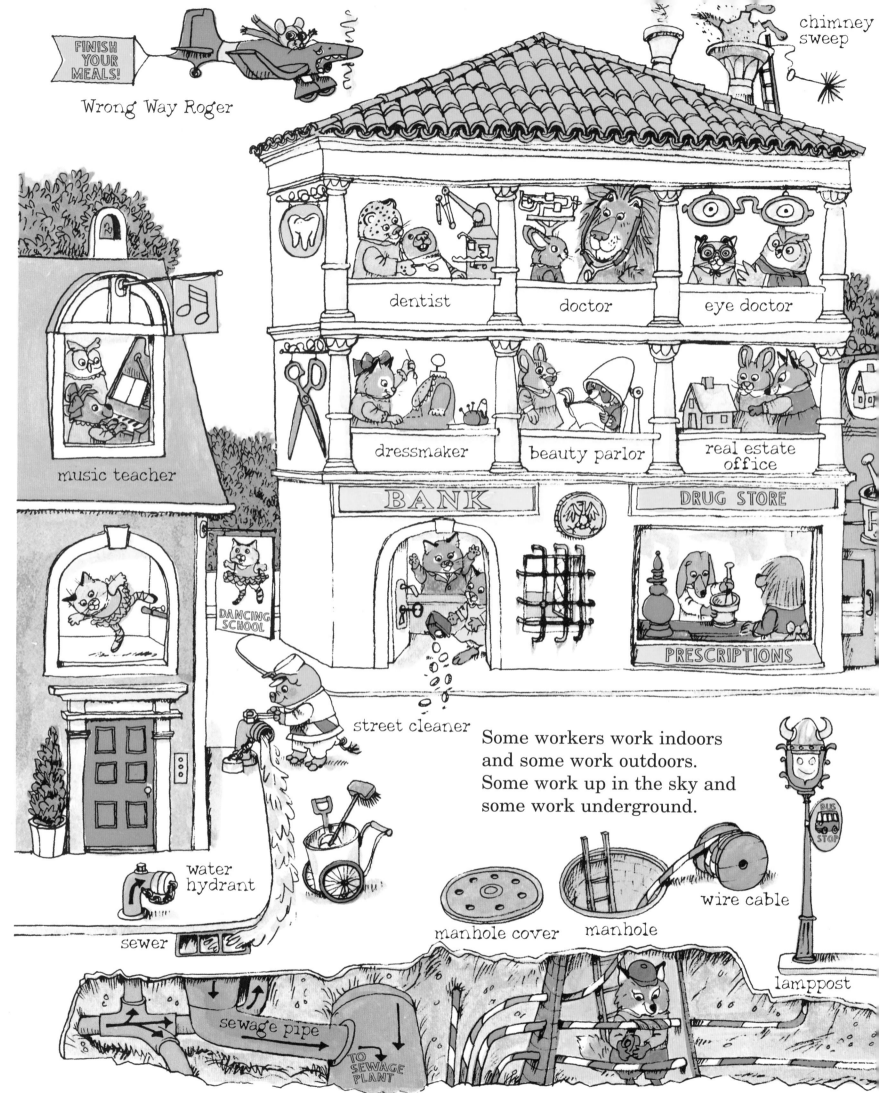

FINISH YOUR MEALS!

Wrong Way Roger

chimney sweep

dentist

doctor

eye doctor

dressmaker

beauty parlor

real estate office

music teacher

DANCING SCHOOL

BANK

DRUG STORE

PRESCRIPTIONS

street cleaner

Some workers work indoors and some work outdoors. Some work up in the sky and some work underground.

BUS STOP

water hydrant

wire cable

manhole cover

manhole

sewer

lamppost

sewage pipe

TO SEWAGE PLANT

6

All kinds of pipes and wires are buried underground.

a stuck truck

a sleeping fireman

FIRE HOUSE

RITZ APARTMENTS

HARDWARE

window washer

BARBER SHOP

laundress

delivery boy

AUTOMOBILES

Some workers always do their
work at the same place.

automobile salesman

TELEPHONE
BOOTH

jack
hammer

Others travel from place
to place to do their jobs.

What does your daddy do?
What does your mommy do?

TAXI

TAXI

And what do YOU do?
Are you a good helper?

7

Everyone is a worker

Farmer Alfalfa   Blacksmith Fox   Stitches the tailor   Grocer Cat   Mommy   Huckle

How many workers are there here?
One, two, three, four, five, six.
What do these workers do?

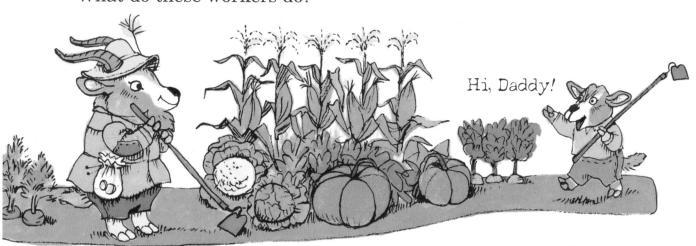

Hi, Daddy!

Farmer Alfalfa grows all kinds of food.
He keeps some of it for his family.

He sells the rest to Grocer Cat
in exchange for money.
Grocer Cat will sell the food
to other people in Busytown.

GROCERIES

potatoes

Today Alfalfa bought a new suit
with some of the money he got
from Grocer Cat.
Stitches, the tailor, makes clothes.
Alfalfa bought his new suit from Stitches.

Then Alfalfa went to Blacksmith Fox's
shop. He had saved enough money
to buy a new tractor. The new tractor
will make his farm work easier.
With it he will be able to grow
more food than he could grow before.
He also bought some presents for
Mommy and his son, Alfred.

Alfalfa put the rest of the money
in the bank for safekeeping.
Then he drove home to his family.

Mommy loved her new earrings.
Alfred loved his present, too.

9

What did the other workers do
with the money they earned?

First they bought food to eat
and clothes to wear.
Then, they put some of the money
in the bank. Later they will use
the money in the bank
to buy other things.

What else did they buy?

Stitches bought an egg beater
so that his family could make fudge.
Try not to get any on your new clothes!

How do I look?

Blacksmith Fox bought more iron
for his shop.
He will heat and bend the metal
to make more tractors and tools.

Grocer Cat bought a new dress for Mommy.
She earned it by taking such good care
of the house.
He also bought a present for his son, Huckle.
Huckle was a very good helper today.

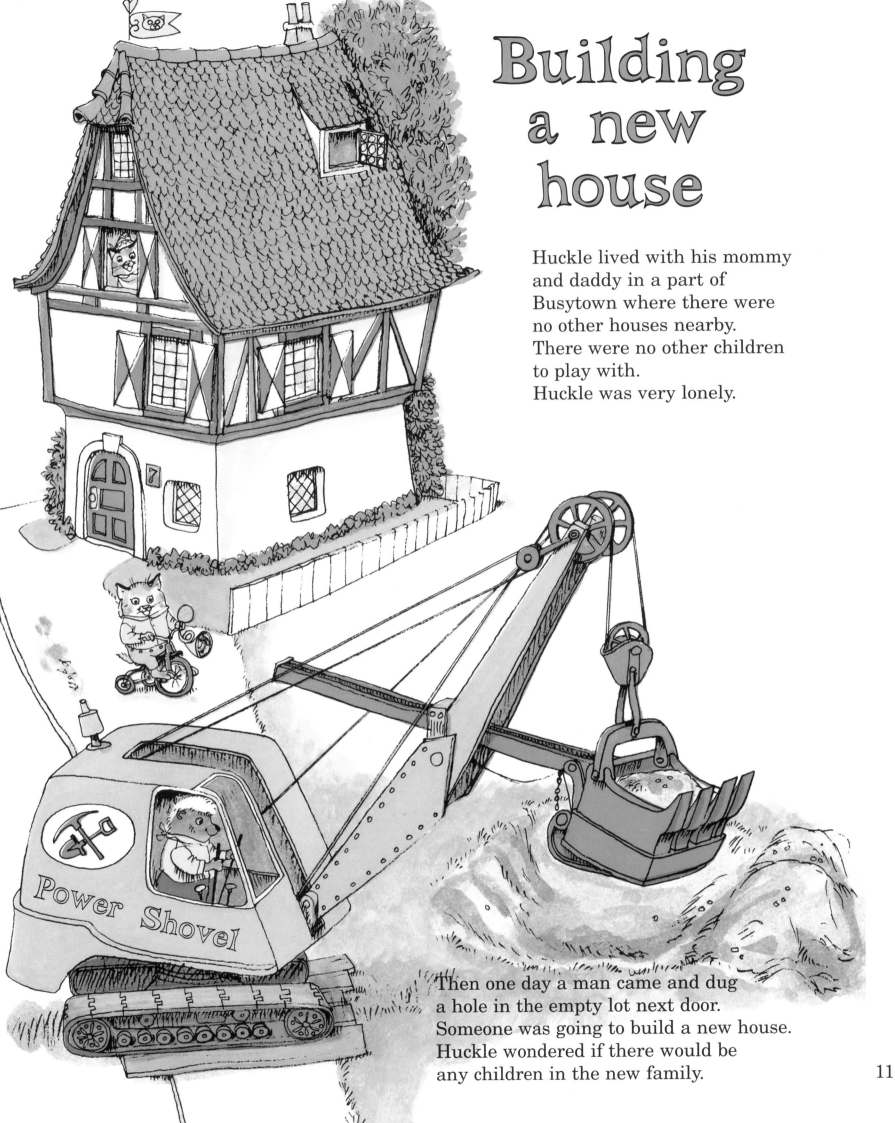

Building a new house

Huckle lived with his mommy
and daddy in a part of
Busytown where there were
no other houses nearby.
There were no other children
to play with.
Huckle was very lonely.

Then one day a man came and dug
a hole in the empty lot next door.
Someone was going to build a new house.
Huckle wondered if there would be
any children in the new family.

11

Jason, the mason, made a foundation
in the hole for the house to be built on.
His helper mixed cement
to hold the bricks together.

Sawdust, the carpenter, and his helpers
started to build the frame of the house.
Jason started to build a chimney.

I wonder if any children
will live there?

Jake, the plumber, attached the water
and sewer pipes to the main pipes
under the street.

Put the bathtub here ↓

hot air duct

hot air duct

cold air return

fuel tank

hot water heater

furnace

ON OFF

CLEAN WATER →
← DIRTY WATER

It's a nice house for children!

They put in water pipes.
They put in sinks and bathtubs and toilets.
They put in a furnace to keep the house warm.
They nailed down floors.
And Jason built the chimney higher.

13

Jason finished making the chimney.
Be careful you don't fall, Jason!

electricity and telephone utility pole

fuse box

NEVER, NEVER
TOUCH!

14

They put a roof and sides on the house.
The electrician put in electric wires.
All kinds of telephones were put in.

The electrician attached electric
switches and outlets to the wires.

Sawdust nailed up the inside walls.
The walls covered up all the pipes and wires.

He put windows
where they belonged—and doors, too.

The house was painted
inside and outside.

clothes washer

stove

refrigerator

sink

A truck brought furniture, a television set,
a radio, rugs, pictures, a stove, and lots of other
things. The house was ready for the new family.

At last the new family has arrived!
Look! It is Stitches, the tailor!
Stitches paid the workmen for
building the house.

bag of money

15

And here is Stitches's family.
"Look, children," said Mother Stitches.
"We have found a new playmate for you."
And Huckle was never lonesome after that.

Mailing a letter

Betsy Bear wrote a letter to Grandma to wish her a Happy Birthday.

She went to the post office to mail it.

She bought an airmail stamp and stuck it on the envelope.

She put the letter in the letter slot.

The postmen stamp all the letters with an inked postmark stamp.

The ink postmark tells you the name of the town that the letter was mailed from. The address shows where the letter is to go.

127,963
127,964

17

Uncle Benny, the postmaster,
read the address on each letter.
All the neighboring towns have
cubbyholes in Busytown Post Office.
Uncle Benny put all the letters
that were going to Grandma's town
in one cubbyhole. He put the letters
going to other towns in
different cubbyholes.

Then he put all the letters
that were going to Grandma's
town in a mailbag.

He took it to Busytown Airport
and put it on an airplane.

EAT AT
JOE'S

Off to Grandma's town the airplane flew.

A postman was waiting at the airport.
He took the mailbag to Grandma's
Post Office.

He read the address on each letter
to see to what part of town it was
to be sent. Each letter carrier
delivers letters to a different
part of town.

North side of town

South side of town

East side of town

West side of town

Soon the bag of Zip, the letter carrier,
was stuffed full. There was no more room
for the last letter, so he put it in his hat.

STOP! STOP!
Where is my birthday letter?

Sorry, Grandma.

Grandma was waiting for a birthday letter from Betsy.

But Zip walked right past her house! He said he didn't have a letter for Grandma in his bag.

She asked him to please look again. So he did.

No! Sorry! No letter for Grandma. He tipped his hat "Good-bye" —and a letter fell out! It was Besty's letter to Grandma!

"Why, Zip! You dear postman!" she said. "You DID bring me a letter from my granddaughter after all!"

She was so happy that she gave Zip a big kiss. Grandmothers just LOVE to get letters from their grandchildren!

Happy Birthday, Grandma
Love and
Kisses xxx
Betsy

Mother's work is never done

Good morning! Good morning!
The sun is up! Everybody up!
Wash! Brush! Comb! Dress!

Get up!
There is a lot of work to be done!

Mommy cooked breakfast. Sally helped her serve it.

Daddy gave Mommy money to buy groceries.
Mommy gave Daddy a kiss as he hurried off to work.

Mommy and Sally and Harry washed the dishes
—and the kitchen floor.

They made the beds.

They cleaned the house.

They drove to the grocery store
to buy food and other things
that they needed at home.

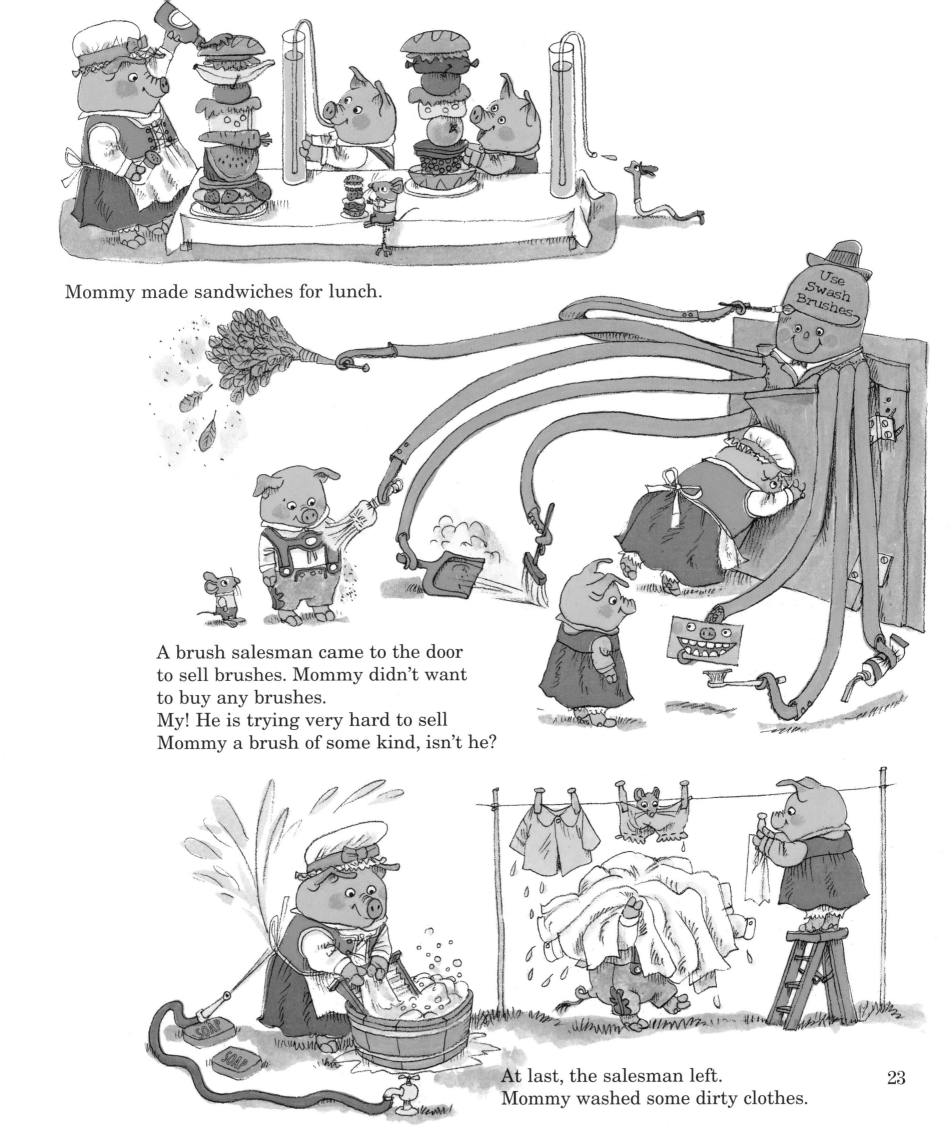

Mommy made sandwiches for lunch.

A brush salesman came to the door
to sell brushes. Mommy didn't want
to buy any brushes.
My! He is trying very hard to sell
Mommy a brush of some kind, isn't he?

At last, the salesman left.
Mommy washed some dirty clothes.

23

Sally and Harry helped Mommy prepare supper.

Daddy came home from work
and kissed everyone.

They sat down to supper.
Daddy should know better than
to try to take such a big bite.

After supper Mommy gave
Sally and Harry a bath.

Daddy weighed himself on the scales.
I think he has eaten too much.

Daddy read a story before bedtime.
He climbed up to kiss Sally goodnight.
Oh dear! I just KNEW he had eaten too much!

Good Night!

Are you all right, Daddy?

I don't think anyone will ever
sleep in that bunk bed again.
Do you?

Sally and Harry had to sleep
with Mommy. What would we
ever do if we didn't have mommies to do
things for us all day—and sometimes all
night? Good night! Sleep tight!

A voyage on a ship

Captain Salty and his crew are getting
their ship ready for a voyage.
The ship will carry passengers to visit
their friends in a faraway land
across the ocean.

26

At last the ship is loaded with
the food and other things they
will need on the long trip.
Here come the passengers!

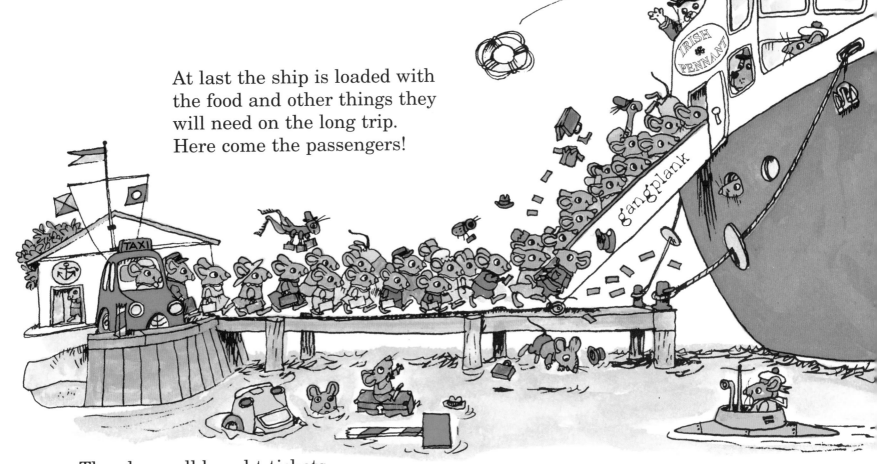

They have all bought tickets
for the trip. They give the tickets to the
purser before they can go aboard the ship. NO PUSHING PLEASE!

light buoy

Tooooooooooot!
It is sailing time. A tiny tugboat pushes
the big ocean liner away from the pier.
Bon voyage! The big ship sails out of the harbor.

27

Soon it is crossing the wide ocean.
There is no land in sight.
Just look at all the things that
happen on an ocean-going ship!

mast

radio aerial

stowaway

lifeboat

stern

deck
steward

stateroom

a gift for Mommy

playroom

dining room

kitchen

cook

crew's quarters

rudder

propeller shaft

fuel oil
tank

The engine turns the propeller. This
makes the ship move through the water.

crow's nest

funnel

air intake

IRISH PENNANT

STOP SLOW SLOW HALF HALF FULL FULL

wheelhouse

chart room

smoke

hospital

engine room

STOP SLOW SLOW HALF HALF FULL FULL

smoke exhaust pipe

MAIL

anchor

cargo hatch

bow

baggage hold

Captain Salty and the crew work hard. They want all the passengers to have a safe and pleasant journey.

Captain Salty lets the engineer in the engine room know when he wants the ship to go fast
—or go slow
—or stop.

The helmsman steers the ship from the wheelhouse.

Suddenly—
the lookout in the crow's nest shouts, "STORM CLOUDS AHEAD!"

The storm hits the ship with great fury!
The radio operator hears someone calling
on the radio.
"SOS! HELP! SAVE US! OUR BOAT IS SINKING!"

Look! There it is!
It's a small fishing boat in trouble!

"FULL SPEED AHEAD!"
roars Captain Salty.
My, the sea is rough!

LOWER THE LIFEBOAT!
Hurry! Hurry! The fishing boat is sinking!
Sailors Miff and Mo row to the rescue.

Bye Bye Boat!

The boat sinks, but the fishermen are safe.

porthole

It's delicious!

Back on board the line, Captain Salty
gives a party to celebrate the rescue.
Will the storm never stop?

LAND HO!!!

Then, just as suddenly as it started,
the storm is over and the sea is calm.
The ship continues on its journey.

Land ho! They have reached
the other side of the ocean.

Everyone thanks the captain and crew for such
an exciting voyage. Then they go ashore to visit friends.
Other people have been waiting to cross the ocean
to visit friends in Busytown. I wonder if their
voyage will be as exciting as this one was?

DEPARTURES BUILDING

ARRIVALS BUILDING

CUSTOMS OFFICE

IN

TO THE BOAT

No pushing please!

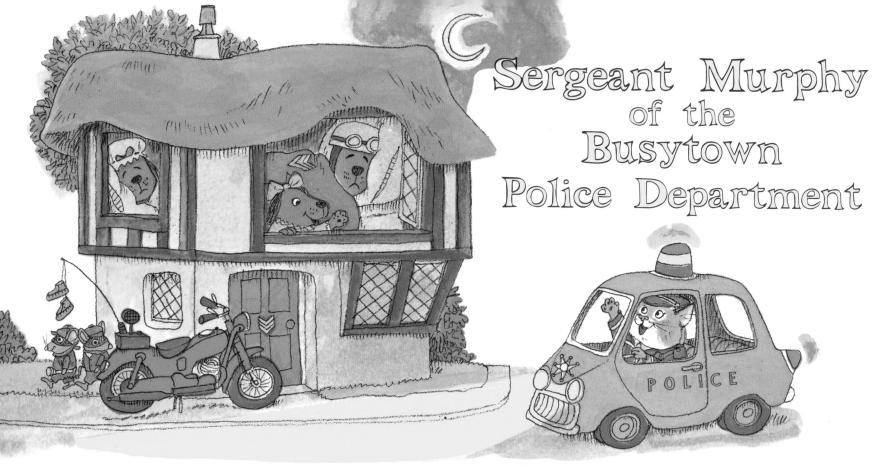

Sergeant Murphy
of the
Busytown
Police Department

Policemen are working at all times to keep things safe and peaceful.
While Sergeant Murphy is sleeping, Policeman Louie is awake.
He will protect the townspeople from harm.

Good Morning!
Sleep Tight!

In the morning, Officer Louie
goes home to bed and
Sergeant Murphy gets up.
Now Sergeant Murphy
will watch out
for everyone's safety.

At the Police Station
the police chief tells
Murphy to drive around
town on his motorcycle.
The chief can talk to
Murphy over the radio
if he has something
important to tell him.

RADIO ROOM

Keep everything peaceful!

CHIEF

HELP! HELP!
My little Huckle
is drowning!

First, Murphy saves Huckle from drowning in the fountain.

Be peaceful!

Then he has to stop two bad boys from fighting.
Look, Murphy! There are two more!

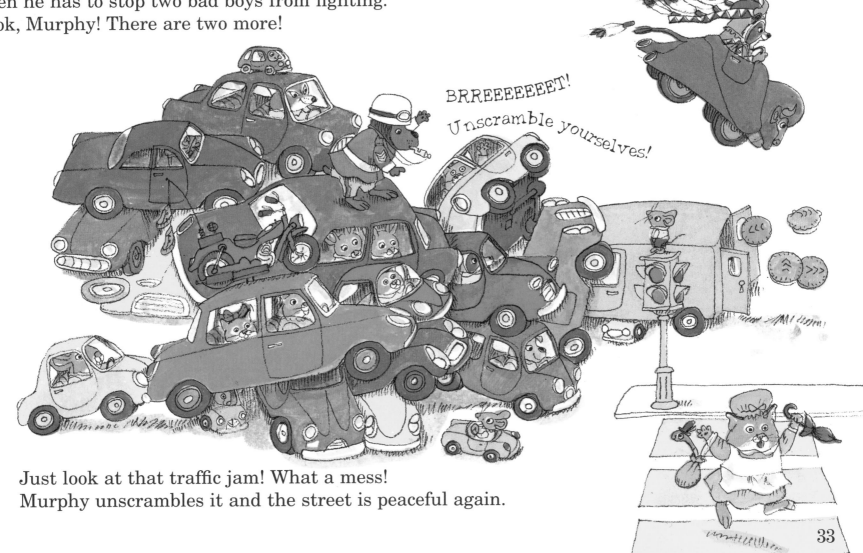

BRREEEEEEET!
Unscramble yourselves!

Just look at that traffic jam! What a mess!
Murphy unscrambles it and the street is peaceful again.

33

He puts parking tickets on cars that are parked where they are not supposed to be.

O Ho! Wild Bill Hiccup and his Buffalomobile! He's speeding again!

Did you see that speeder hit Murphy's motorcycle? Chase him, Murphy!

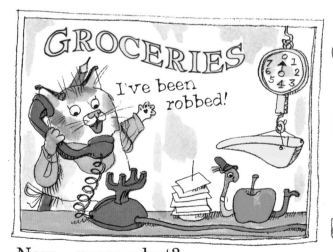

Try to be good!

Murphy gives him a speeding ticket. For punishment he will not be allowed to drive his Buffalomobile for a few days. Let that be a lesson to you, Wild Bill Hiccup!

Now—guess what? Grocer Cat telephones the Police Station. A robber has stolen some bananas from the grocery store.

The chief of police calls Murphy over the radio. "CATCH THE THIEF!" he says.

34

Catch the thief!

Look, Murphy! There's the thief now!
It's Gorilla Bananas!

Catch the thief!

Murphy chases after him.
OOPS! His motorcycle slipped
on a banana peel. It is good
that he is wearing a crash helmet.

CLONK!

He has captured Bananas!

The paddy wagon comes to take Bananas to jail.
He will stay there until he learns that
it is wrong to steal things from others.

Nice work, Murphy!

It is time for Murphy to stop working.
Now he can go home for supper with his family.
Policeman Louie wakes up. He will keep
everything peaceful during the night.

In the middle of the night,
Louie hears a loud crying noise.
If the noise doesn't stop
it will wake up everyone in town.
Why, it is Bridget, Murphy's little girl!
WAKE UP, MURPHY! BRIDGET IS HUNGRY!

Murphy has to get up and warm
a bottle of milk for Bridget.
Bridget stops crying.

Sergeant Murphy really knows
how to keep Busytown safe and peaceful.
Doesn't he?

Firemen to the rescue

FIRE!
Mother Cat was ironing
one of Daddy's shirts.
The iron was too hot.
The shirt began to burn.
"FIRE!" she shouted.

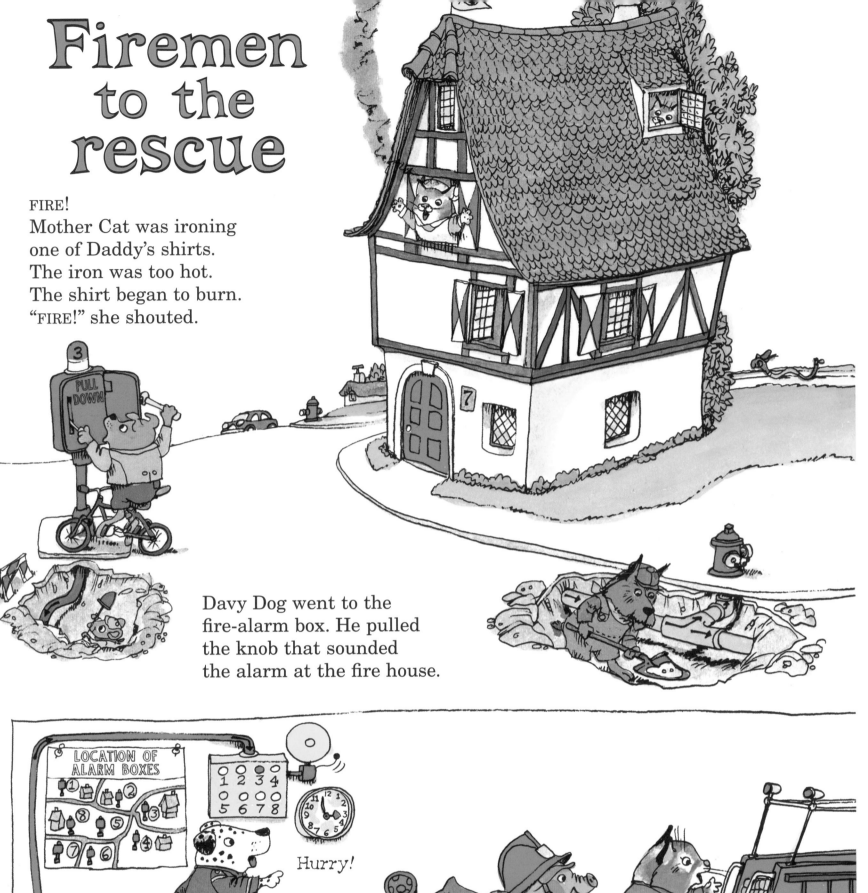

Davy Dog went to the
fire-alarm box. He pulled
the knob that sounded
the alarm at the fire house.

Firemen are at the fire house
at all times. They have to be
ready to put fires out quickly.

As soon as the alarm rang,
they ran to their fire engines.
HURRY!

Clang! Clang! Clang!
The firemen rushed to the fire.
They raised the ladder on the ladder truck.
A fireman ran up the ladder to rescue Mommy.
"SAVE MY HUCKLE!" she screamed.

Save Huckle too!

water hydrant

Water is used to put fires out.
The water runs through pipes under the street.
The firemen attached a hose between the
water hydrant and the pumper engine.
The pumper engine got water from the hydrant
and squirted it out through the hose nozzle.

But the ladder wasn't
long enough to reach Huckle
up in the playroom!
How will they ever save him?

"SAVE MY HUCKLE!" screamed Mommy Cat
as the firemen carried her down.

Smokey came running to the house.
He had a smoke mask so that
he would be able to breathe
in the smoke-filled house.

He also had a
special ladder.

He climbed up the
fire-truck ladder
as far as he could.
He reached up with
his special ladder
and hooked it over
the window sill. Then he
climbed up.
He just had to
rescue Huckle!

40

The playroom door was closed.
Smokey chopped it down with his ax.

He picked up Huckle—
and he jumped out the window!

PLOPP!
Sparky and Snozzle were ready
just in time to catch them
in the life net.
Daddy arrived just in time
to see Smokey save Huckle.

At last the fire was out.
Look at poor Daddy's shirt!
But that doesn't matter.
The firemen have saved
his family and his house.
That is much more important!

The firemen went back to the fire house.
They hung the wet hose up to dry.
They put a fresh, dry hose on the trucks.
They have to be ready to fight fires
ALL OF THE TIME!
Brave firemen are always ready
to protect us and our homes from fire.

Hey!
Smokey!
Why didn't you
just OPEN the
playroom door?

A visit to the hospital

Mommy took Abby to visit Doctor Lion.
He looked at her tonsils.
"Hmmmm. Very bad tonsils," he said.
"I shall have to take them out.
Meet me at the hospital tomorrow."

On the next day, Daddy drove them to the hospital.
Abby waved to the ambulance driver.
Ambulances bring people to hospitals
if they have to get there in a hurry.

Nurse Nelly was waiting for Abby.
Mommy had to go home, but she
promised to bring Abby a present
after the doctor had taken her
tonsils out.

43

Nurse Nelly took Abby up to the children's room.

Roger Dog was in the bed next to hers.
His tonsils were already out.
He was eating a big dish of ice cream.

Nurse Nelly put Abby on the bed.
She pulled a curtain around them.
No one could see what was going on.

Why, she was helping Abby
put on a nightgown!

Doctor Lion peeked into the room.
He told Nurse Nelly he was going
to put on his operating clothes.
He told Nurse Nelly to bring
Abby to the operating room.

Off to the operating room they went.
Doctor Lion was waiting there.
Everyone but the patient wears
a face mask in the operating room
so that germs won't spread.

Doctor Lion told Abby that she
was going to go to sleep.
He said she would stay asleep
until her tonsils were out.

Doctor Dog put a mask
over her nose and mouth.
She breathed in and out.
In an instant she was asleep.

When she woke up she found
herself back in the bed next
to Roger's. Her tonsils were all gone!
Her throat was sore, but it felt better
after she had some ice cream.

Whoooooeeee!
Abby saw her mommy arriving
in the ambulance.
Abby thought her mother must be
in a hurry to see her.

45

She waited and waited
—but Mommy didn't come.
At last Doctor Lion came.
"Your mother has brought you
a present," he said.
He took Abby for a ride
in a wheelchair.

"There is your present," he said.
"It is your new baby brother!
Your mom just gave birth to
him here in the hospital."
Then they all went to Mommy's
room in the hospital.
Daddy was there, too.

He looks like me, don't you think?

What a lucky girl she was!
She left her tonsils
at the hospital,
but she brought home
a cute baby brother.

46

But remember! Very few children receive such
a nice present when they have their tonsils out!

The train trip

The Pig family is going on a train
to visit their cousins in a town far away.
They will travel all day and all night to get there.

Daddy buys train tickets
at the railroad station.

Mommy buys books
and magazines to read.

A porter takes their bags
to the train.

This old train has a steam locomotive.
It is only going to make
a short trip to the next town.
The Pig family will ride
overnight on another train.

47

Wait!

HALT!

SLEEPING CAR

DINING CAR

MILK

FLOUR

EGGS

Their train has a sleeping car
with separate rooms for each family.
These rooms are called compartments.
At night, the seats will be made into beds.
Look! There is Huckle's family.

Food and water are brought to
the kitchen in the dining car.
The cook will cook their meals.
The waiter will serve them.

ALL ABOOOOOARD!
It is time to leave.
The train rolls out of the station.
The signal light tells the engineer
that there is a clear track ahead.
He doesn't want to bump into another train.

GANDY
DANCERS'
BALL

COMING
SOON

STOP

GO

signal tower

48

Mailbags and heavy baggage
are put on the train.
Some of it will be delivered
to stations along the way.

The locomotive needs fuel oil
to make its motors go.
The motors turn the wheels so that
the train can roll along the railroad track.

The switchman can
switch the train
from one track to another.
If he makes a mistake
the train won't go
to the right place.

The conductor collects the
tickets. The tickets show that
Daddy has paid for the trip.

In Huckle's compartment, the porter
is getting the pillows and
blankets ready for bedtime.

It is time to eat dinner.
Cookie has already made the soup.
He is trying to flip the pancakes
from the side that is cooked
to the side that is not cooked.
You are not doing very well, Cookie!

The mailman delivers a bag of
mail to the railroad station of
a town they are passing through.

The watchman lowers the crossing
gates before a train crosses a road.
He doesn't want any cars to
bump into the train.
But Wild Bill Hiccup
just HAS to bump into something!

51

Oh dear!
The train has swerved and the
waiter has spilled the soup!

While they are eating,
the porter changes
their seats into beds.

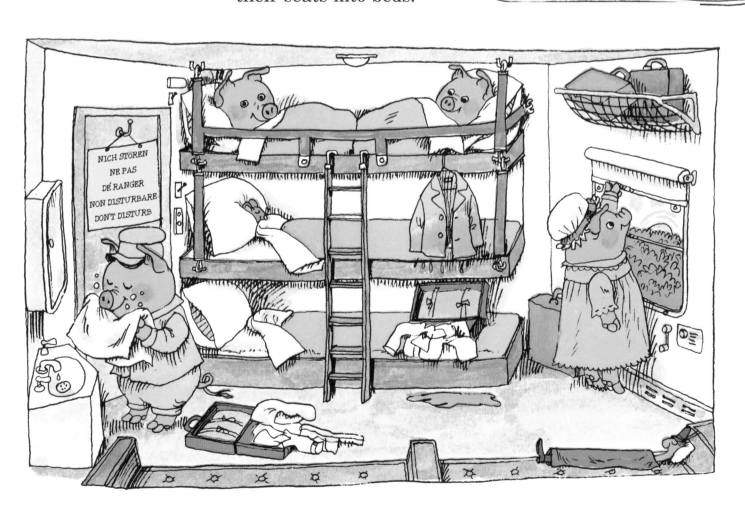

After dinner, everyone gets ready for bed.

Clickety clack, clickety clack.
The train speeds on through the night.
The train crew won't go to sleep
until the trip is over.
Cookie is still trying to learn how to
flip pancakes. Keep trying, Cookie.

WIENER SCHNITZEL

ICE CREAM CAR

It is morning when they
arrive at their cousins' town.
Their cousins are at the
railroad station to greet them.
I think they will have fun
on their visit. Don't you?

53

The story of seeds
and how they grow

Farmer Alfalfa grows all kinds of vegetables on his farm.

Best of all, he likes to grow sweet, sweet corn.

Last summer when it was time to plant corn, Alfalfa poured the bag of corn seeds into the corn planter. Don't spill!

He planted the seeds in straight rows in his cornfield.

The hot sun shone down and after a while, tiny green plants popped up. The corn was starting to grow.

Rain fell on the plants. Soon ears of corn grew on the cornstalks.

Then—after many days of sun and rain—
Alfalfa opened an ear of corn.
He wanted to see if his field of corn
was ready to be picked.
It was! The corn was ripe and ready for eating.

Alfalfa drove his corn picker
back and forth across his cornfield.
The ears of corn were picked from
the stalks and dumped into a wagon.

Each ear of corn has many seed kernels.
Alfalfa knew that he would need seeds to plant
at the next corn-planting time.
So he put some corn kernels in a bag
to save for planting.
He kept some ears to eat himself.

55

He put the rest in his
little old truck to sell to Grocer Cat.
My! His truck is falling apart!

Well, that's the end of THAT truck!
Grocer Cat gave money to Alfalfa for the corn.

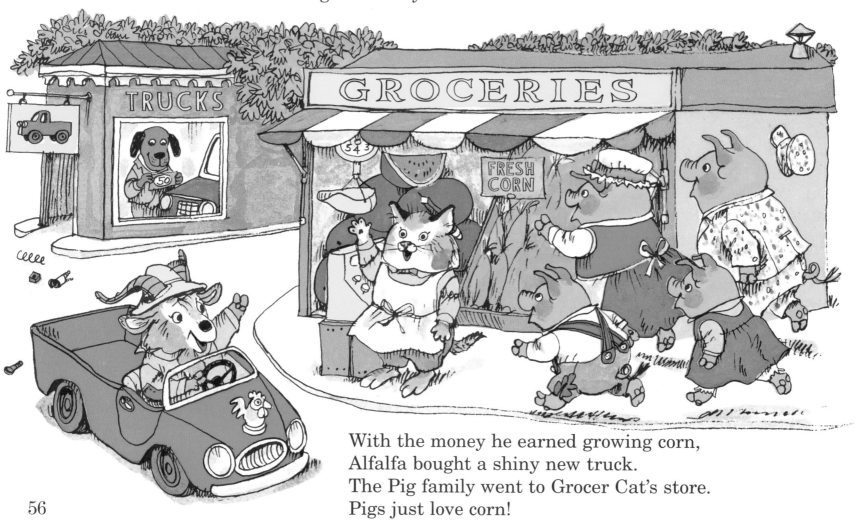

With the money he earned growing corn,
Alfalfa bought a shiny new truck.
The Pig family went to Grocer Cat's store.
Pigs just love corn!

They bought lots of corn and took it home for supper.

They ate and ate and ate
until there was no more left
—except one tiny little seed corn!
Mommy Pig said to Harry,
"FINISH YOUR SUPPER!"

Harry asked if he could plant
the last tiny seed instead of
eating it. Mommy agreed.
He planted the seed in the earth.
The sun shone hot and the rain fell cool.
After a while, a tiny green plant popped up.
The plant grew and grew and grew.

One day Alfalfa came to visit.
"My goodness," he said.
"Harry has grown the best
corn I have ever seen.
I am sure he will grow up
to be a very good farmer!"
Harry was very pleased.

The airplane ride

Huckle was going to fly on an airplane
with his mommy and daddy.
They were going to visit Grandma.
They took a bus to the airport.

Daddy bought tickets
from the ticket seller.

They checked in their bags at the ticket desk.
The bags were sent to the cargo hold of the airplane.

The ground crew was busy getting
the airplane ready to fly.
The family went up to the
observation deck to watch them.

The weatherman and the flight dispatcher
told the flight crew which part of the sky
to fly in on the way to Grandma's.

When the plane was almost ready,
the flight crew climbed aboard the plane.

Then the passengers got on board.
After the door was closed, the ground
crew took the stairs away.

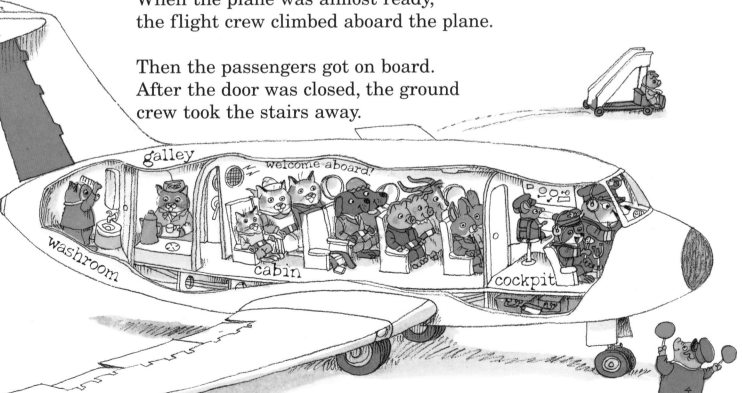

galley

welcome aboard!

washroom

cabin

cockpit

The pilot called the control tower on the radio.
He said that he was ready to take off.

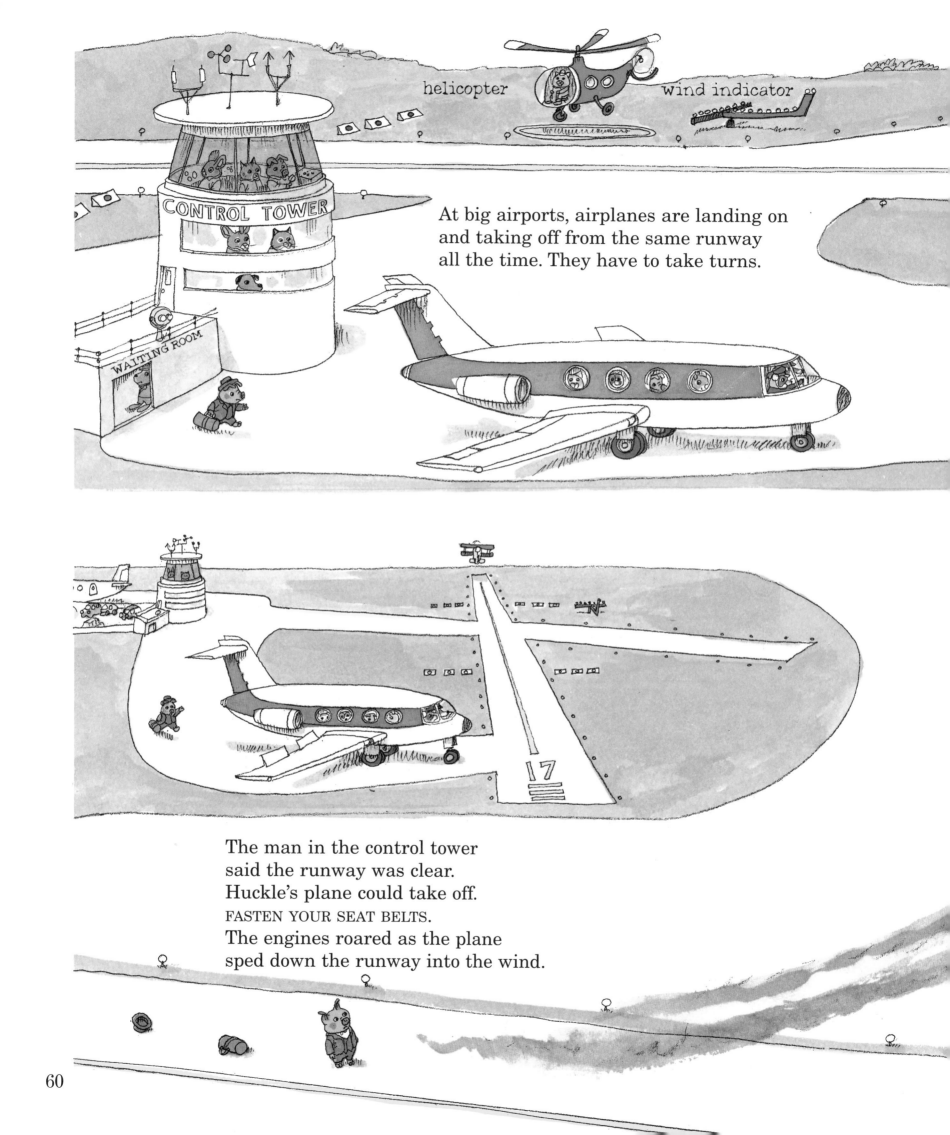

helicopter

wind indicator

CONTROL TOWER

WAITING ROOM

At big airports, airplanes are landing on
and taking off from the same runway
all the time. They have to take turns.

17

The man in the control tower
said the runway was clear.
Huckle's plane could take off.
FASTEN YOUR SEAT BELTS.
The engines roared as the plane
sped down the runway into the wind.

runway

taxiway

The plane rose gently off the ground.
The pilot pushed a button and
the wheels folded up into the plane.
Up, up, up, it flew.

61

The pilot used radar
to find where the best flying weather was.
Huckle's plane flew high above the clouds.

The stewardess brought
a book for Huckle to read.

She served a delicious
meal to everyone.

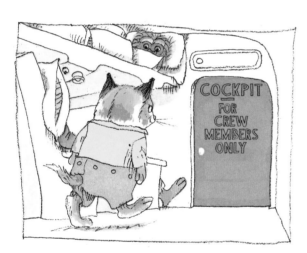

Huckle was curious to see
what was in the cockpit.
STOP! YOU'RE NOT SUPPOSED
TO GO IN THERE!

Too late! The pilot had started to land.
Everyone was too busy to take Huckle back to his seat.
The pilot talked on the radio to the control tower.
He was told that the runway was clear for landing.

The pilot slowed down the plane.
He circled around and around—lower and lower.

Burblll! Thunk! The pilot lowered
the landing wheels into place.
Hang on tight, Huckle!
You don't have a seat belt on.
Now, let's come in for a perfect landing.

Why, there's Grandma!
She could see Huckle in the pilot's cockpit.

Grandma rushed up to the airplane
after it had landed safely.
"Why, Huckle!" she said. "When did you learn how to
fly an airplane? Will you teach me how?"
Maybe someday he will.

63

Wood
and how we use it

We couldn't live without trees.
We get wood from trees.
We use wood in many ways.
Let's see how we get our wood.

TIMBER!

The lumberjack cuts down the tree.

The branches are cut
off the tree trunk.

The tree trunk is sawed into logs.

tree
trunk

a seed

a one-year-old tree

log

This tree is almost 100 years old
and is ready to be cut down.

The logs are put
in a river to
float downstream.

64

The forest ranger watches out
for fires. A forest fire
could burn down a whole forest.

Some trees are left standing.
Seeds from these trees
will fall to the ground.
New trees will grow in place of
the old ones that have been cut down.

The foresters also
scatter seeds from helicopters.

stump

Loggers ride the logs down the river.
They try to keep the logs from getting jammed.
Oh dear! The logs are jammed!
Unscramble that log jam, loggers!

Good work, loggers!
You broke up the log jam.
Now the logs can float to
the sawmill and be sawed into boards.

TOM SAWYER'S SAWMILL

Water falling over
a water wheel makes
all the machinery work.

lumber

lumberyard

SAWDUST THE CARPENTER

BOAT BUILDER

FURNITURE

66

The logs are sawed into rough boards.

The rough wood is sawed into boards of different sizes.

scrap lumber

FOOLSCAP PAPER CO.

straddle truck

The lumber is stacked in the lumberyard to dry. Many kinds of workers come to buy the lumber they need for building things. Daddy Pig has bought some lumber to build a bookcase.

67

The paper makers use scraps
of wood to make paper.

FOOLSCAP PAPER COMPANY

chipper

blower

digester

chemicals

beater

mixer

Wet wood pulp moves onto a wire screen belt.
Water is removed by rollers and dryers.

dry end | drying | paper making machine | wire screen | wet end | wet wood pulp

a finished
roll of paper

ABC PRINTERS

Some paper is used to make bags and boxes.
Some is for making books.
The paper used in this book was taken
to the printing shop where books are made.
The printer puts the words
and pictures on the pages.

The boat builder uses curved
pieces of wood to make boats.

BOAT BUILDER

The furniture maker makes beds and chests and chairs.

Carpenters have a custom of nailing a tree branch to the roof of a new house.

Some trees give us fruit.

Harry is planting an apple seed.
An apple tree will grow from the seed.
It will take a long time.
Someday YOU might like to plant a tree.

Trees shade us from the hot sun.

Digging coal to make electricity work for us

steam boiler

FRESH AIR ENTER HERE

Pick! Pick! Pick! Dig! Dig! Dig! The miners dig coal out of the coal mine under the ground.

Water seeps into the mine and has to be pumped out.

Elevators raise and lower the miners and coal cars.

After the coal is dug out, wood timbers are needed to hold up the roof.

coal

The miners use picks and drills to break the coal into small pieces.

The seeping water collects in the sump.

sump

70

BURIED SUNLIGHT COAL MINE

THE TIPPLE

COAL

COAL

DIANE

Many years ago, sunlight poured down
on the plants and trees
and helped them to grow.
When these plants and trees died,
they sank into the ground.
Gradually they were changed into coal.

The coal is brought up out
of the mine to the tipple.
Then it is loaded into
railroad coal cars.

Miners need fresh air.
A fan blows out the stale air
and fresh air rushes in.

The miners blast the
hard, black coal
with explosives.

stale air leaves this way

EXPLOSIVE

The loader loads coal
into small coal cars.

TO THE
TIPPLE

loader

71

By burning coal, we are able to make electricity work for us.
The electricity lights our homes.
That is why we call coal "buried sunlight."
There is electricity in everything. But it is not useful to us until it is moving. Coal helps to make electricity move.

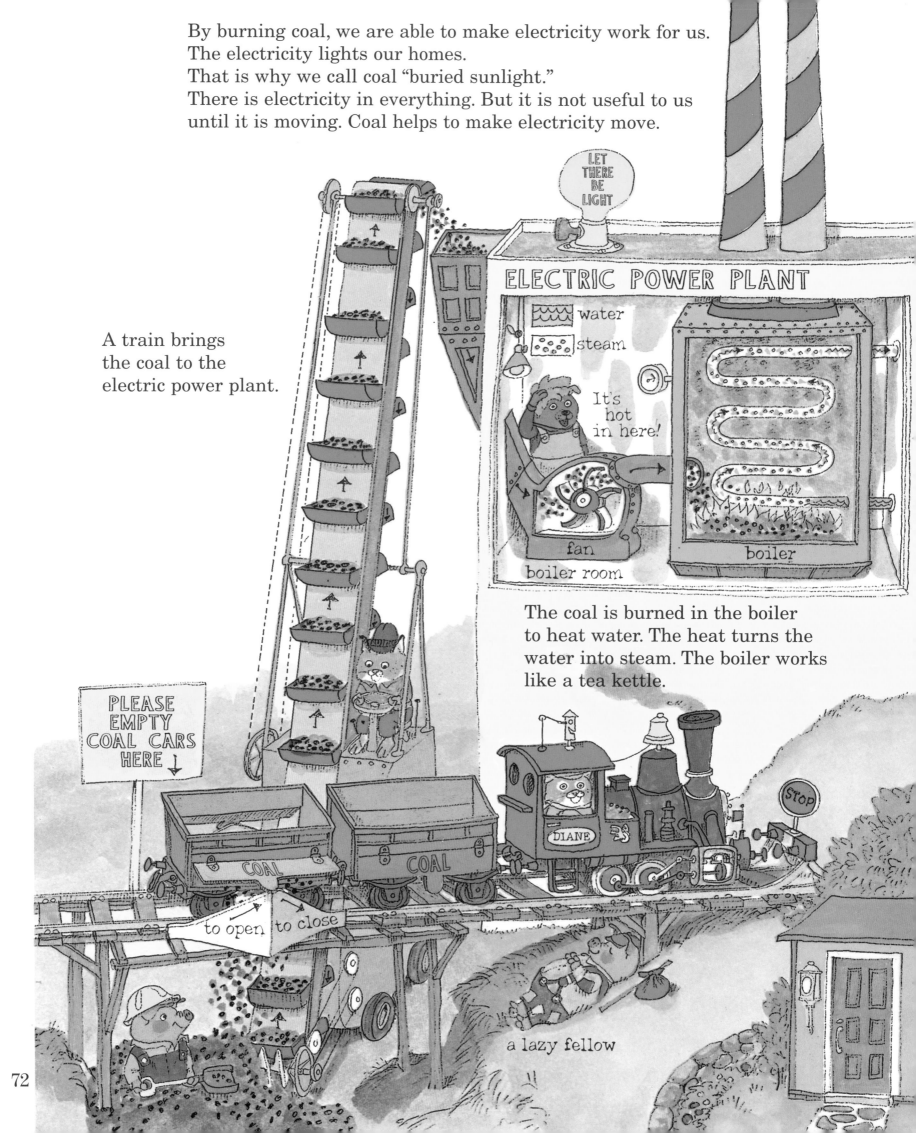

A train brings the coal to the electric power plant.

The coal is burned in the boiler to heat water. The heat turns the water into steam. The boiler works like a tea kettle.

The steam forces the turbine to turn,
just as the wind moves the windmill.
This turbine turns the electric generator
that forces the electricity to move.
This moving electricity is called an electric current.

$$resistance = \frac{potential\ difference}{current}$$

OHM'S LAW

turbine   electric
                generator

the steam is cooled,
and condenses back to water

pump

The electric current travels
through wires into our homes.

substation

Electricity is used in many ways.
But the most important use
of all is to give us light.

meter

main
switch

Building a new road

Good roads are very important to all of us.
Doctors need them to visit patients.
Firemen need them to go to fires.
We all need them to visit one another.
The road between Busytown and Workville
was bumpy and crooked and very dusty—

—except when it rained!
Then the dirt turned to mud and everyone got stuck.

The mayors of the two towns went to the road engineer
and told him that they wanted to have a new road.
The townspeople had agreed to pay the road engineer
and his workers to build the new road.

Get rid of those bumps!
Make this road flat and straight, Bugdozer!

surveying instrument

OK, Chief!

The surveyor used his instruments to make sure that the road would be straight.

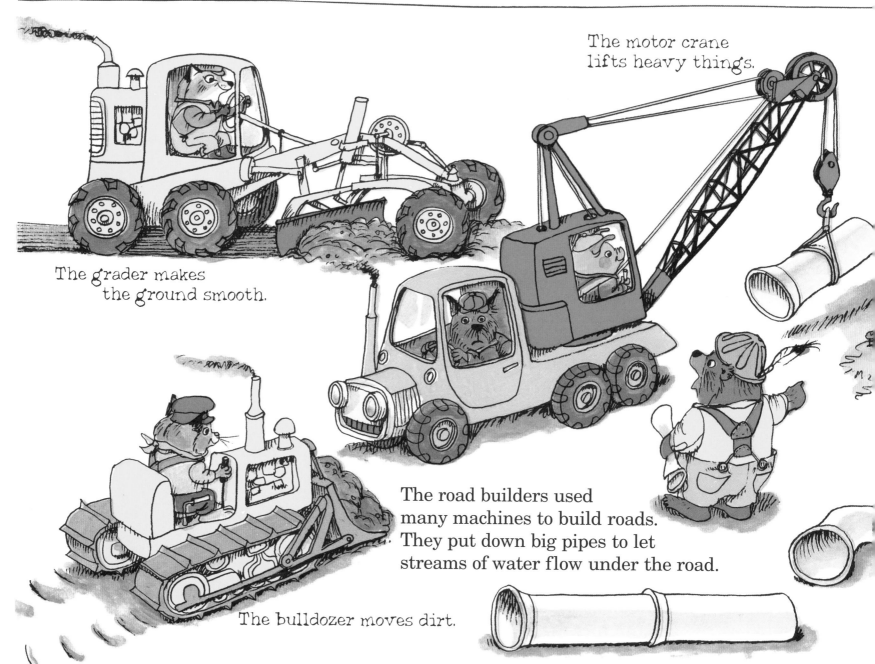

The grader makes the ground smooth.

The motor crane lifts heavy things.

The road builders used many machines to build roads. They put down big pipes to let streams of water flow under the road.

The bulldozer moves dirt.

The surveyor's helpers used stakes and
string to show where the road was to go.

water drainage ditch

tractor shovel

ditch digger

dump truck

At last the roadbed was
straight and smooth.
But it needed a hard top
so that there would be no dust or mud.

77

Big rocks were put into the rock crusher
to be crushed into smaller stones.

A stone spreader spread the stones
evenly over the roadbed.

A truck squirted sticky asphalt oil
on the stones to make them stick together.

The stone cutter shapes
the stones so that they
will fit next to each other.

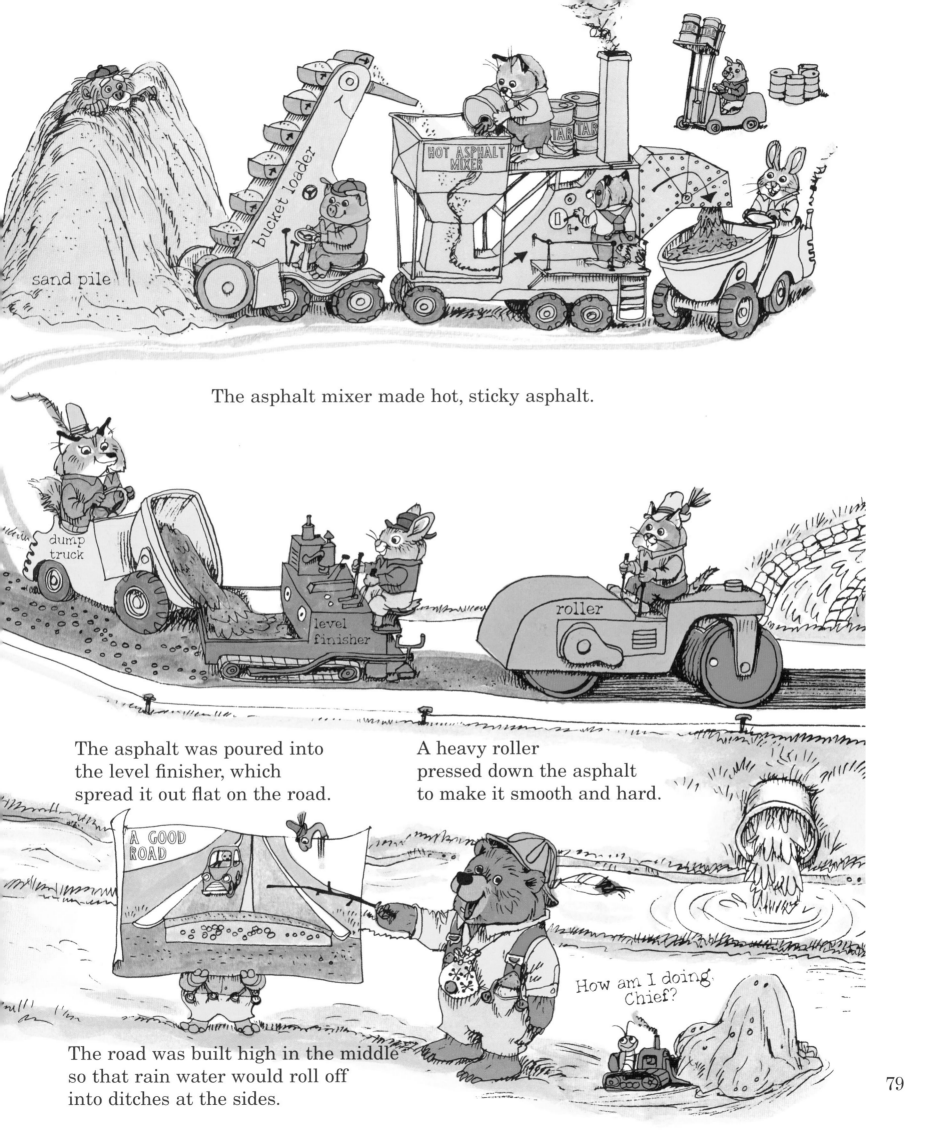

The asphalt mixer made hot, sticky asphalt.

The asphalt was poured into
the level finisher, which
spread it out flat on the road.

A heavy roller
pressed down the asphalt
to make it smooth and hard.

A GOOD
ROAD

How am I doing,
Chief?

The road was built high in the middle
so that rain water would roll off
into ditches at the sides.

79

Street lights were put up so that drivers could see the road clearly at night.

FIREFLY LIGHTING COMPANY

electric cable

SNACK BAR

EAT

GASOLINE

gas pump

GAS AND OIL

DIVIDING LINE PAINTER

gasoline storage tank

OIL

GARDENER

All right, you two fellows! Stop talking and finish covering up that underground gasoline storage tank!

80

The workers put up guard rails
to keep cars from going off the road.

STOP · NO ENTRY · GREEN · 5 · P · DANGER · SIGNS

They posted many signs.
Some signs remind drivers to drive safely.
Some signs show which way to go.

A dividing line painter painted a line down the middle of the road.
Dividing lines remind drivers to keep on their own side.

Don't push!

HELP PREVENT FOREST FIRES

Everyone wanted to be the first
one to drive on the new road.
But Grandma Cat was the first!
Wasn't she lucky?

My Mink

81

Cotton
and how we use it

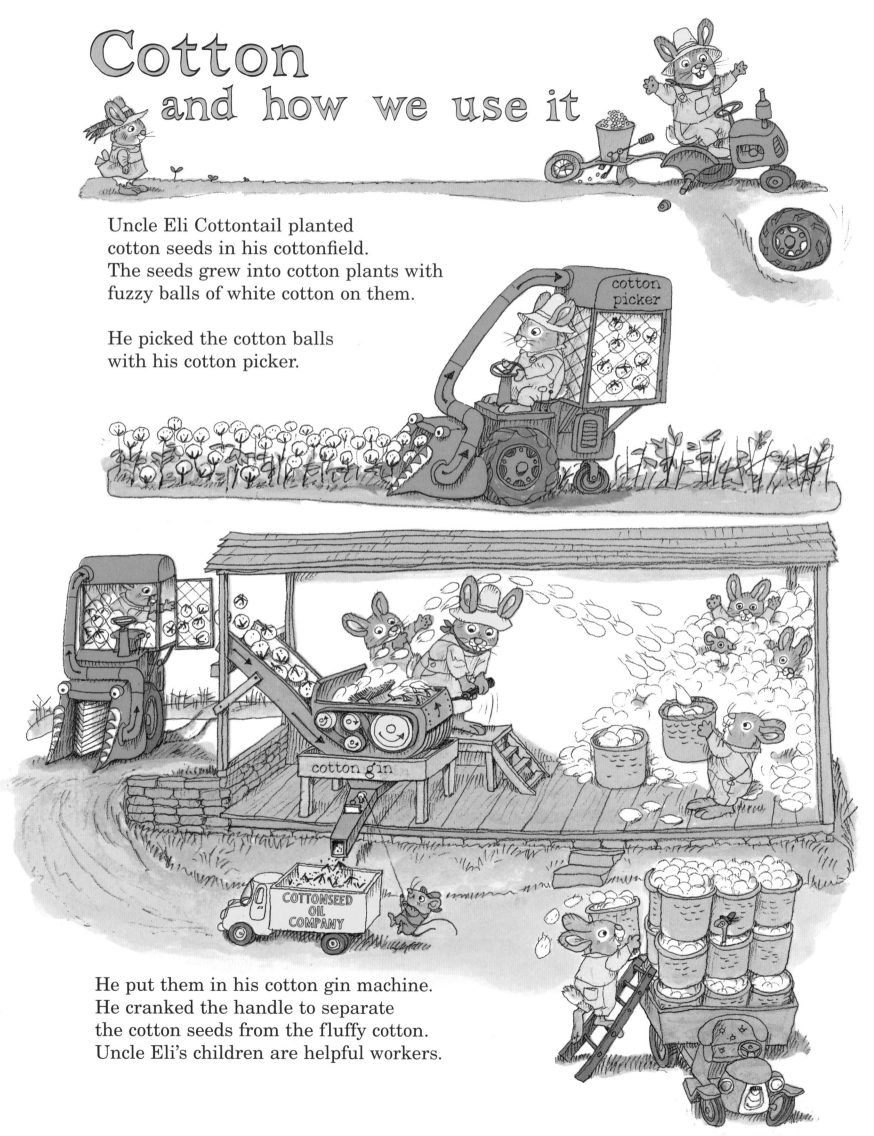

Uncle Eli Cottontail planted
cotton seeds in his cottonfield.
The seeds grew into cotton plants with
fuzzy balls of white cotton on them.

He picked the cotton balls
with his cotton picker.

cotton picker

cotton gin

COTTONSEED OIL COMPANY

He put them in his cotton gin machine.
He cranked the handle to separate
the cotton seeds from the fluffy cotton.
Uncle Eli's children are helpful workers.

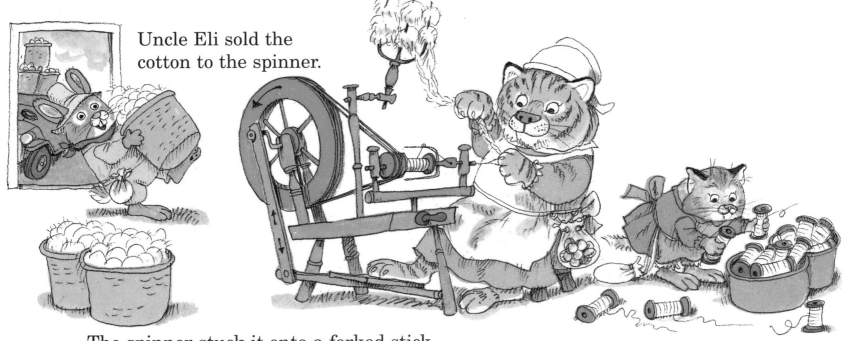

Uncle Eli sold the cotton to the spinner.

The spinner stuck it onto a forked stick.
She pulled a pinch of it and twisted it.
She made her spinning wheel go around.
She wound the twisted cotton thread onto spools.
She spun all the cotton balls into thread.

The threads were sold to the dye works.
The workers put them in a dye vat.
Blue dye in the vat changed the
white thread into a nice blue color.
They hung the blue thread up to dry.

When it was dry the thread was sold to the weavers.

The weavers used a loom to
weave cloth out of thread.
Some threads were put on the warp beam.

Others were wound on spools
and placed in shuttles.

The weaver slid the shuttle back and forth
between the threads that were up, and those that were down.
She changed the up and down threads after each slide.
The threads went over and under each other and made cloth.
OOPS! You slid the shuttle too hard!

The weavers sold the finished
cloth to the clothing makers.

The cutters had paper dress and suit patterns
to show them how to cut the cloth.

Tailors and seamstresses sewed
the pieces of cloth together to make
suits and dresses for boys and girls.
The clothing was put into stores to be sold.

Why, there's Uncle Eli buying clothes for his family!
He is spending the money he earned selling cotton.
Isn't it wonderful that we can make clothes out of plants?

Where bread comes from

grain combine

chaff

wheat field

Farmer Pig gathers his crop of wheat with a harvesting machine. The grain seeds are separated from the stalks and poured into a truck.

wheat grain seeds

bucket loader

The wheat grain seeds are scooped out and put into bags.

Then the seeds are taken to the mill.

86

FLOUR MILL

The bags are hoisted to the top of the mill.

The miller pours the seeds into the hopper.

hopper

The seeds are crushed between the grindstones. Water power turns the top grindstone.

grindstone
turning stone
fixed stone

sharpening a grindstone

Sifters separate the soft flour from the hard shell of the seed.

sifter
bin
bran

FLOUR XXXX

The flour is sewn into bags.

FLOUR XXXX

FLOUR XXXX

Waterwheel

falling water turns the waterwheel

FLOUR XXXX   FLOUR

FLOUR XXXX

The bags are put on a truck that will take them to the Bakery. OOPS!

The bakers will bake the flour into bread.

mixing trough

They mix water and salt and yeast with the flour to make bread dough. It is important to mix the right amounts. The yeast makes the dough puff up. The bakers knead the dough until it is well mixed.

The bakers mold the dough into loaves of many different shapes and sizes.

Able Baker Charlie mixes his own special dough. Isn't he putting too much yeast in his dough?

88

Able Baker Charlie has made teeny tiny loaves.

Baker Fox cleans the hot fire coals out of the ovens.

The loaves are ready to be baked
in the hot oven.
The heat in the oven will make
the loaves puff up even more.

Yoicks!

The bakers play card games while
waiting for the bread to bake.
Oh my! Look at what's happening!
Take out the tiny loaves of bread!

Too late! I think you DID put too much
yeast in your dough, Able Baker Charlie!
Mmmmmmm! But it DOES taste good!

89

Water

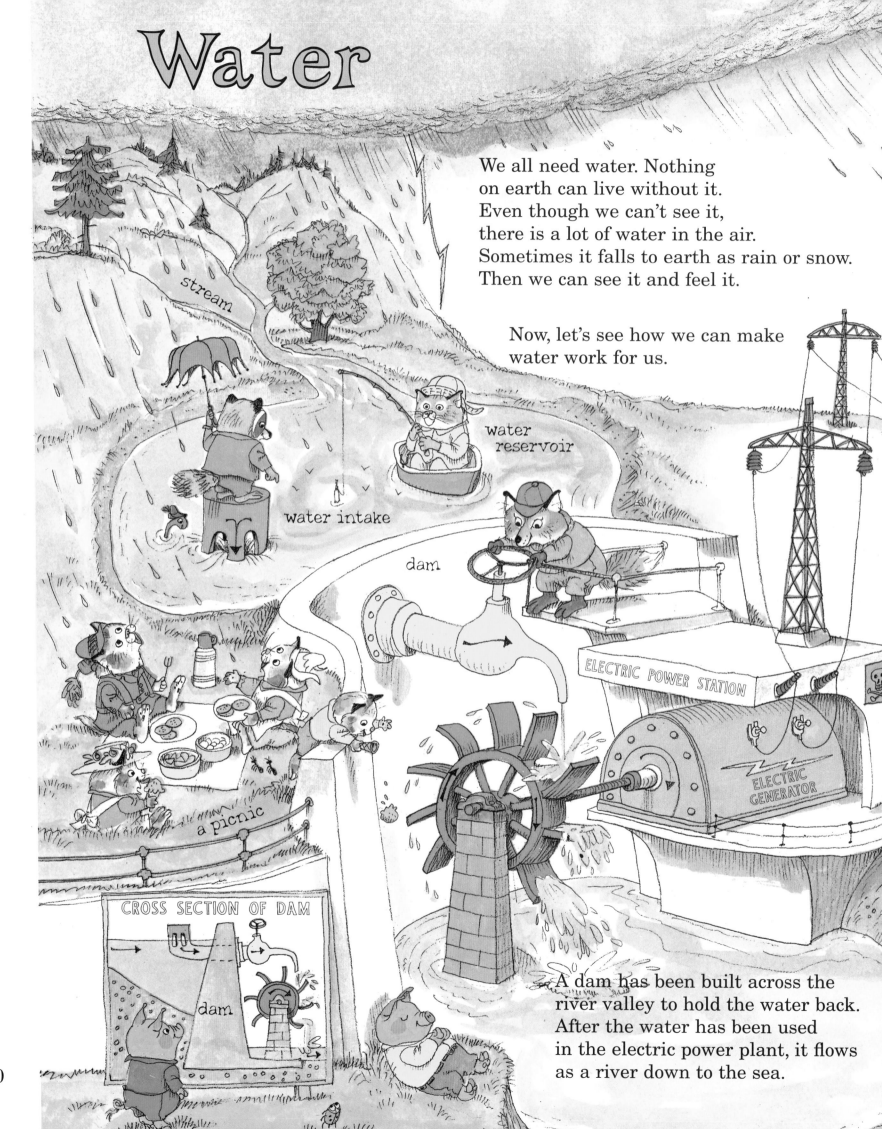

We all need water. Nothing
on earth can live without it.
Even though we can't see it,
there is a lot of water in the air.
Sometimes it falls to earth as rain or snow.
Then we can see it and feel it.

Now, let's see how we can make
water work for us.

stream

water
reservoir

water intake

dam

a picnic

CROSS SECTION OF DAM

dam

ELECTRIC POWER STATION

ELECTRIC
GENERATOR

A dam has been built across the
river valley to hold the water back.
After the water has been used
in the electric power plant, it flows
as a river down to the sea.

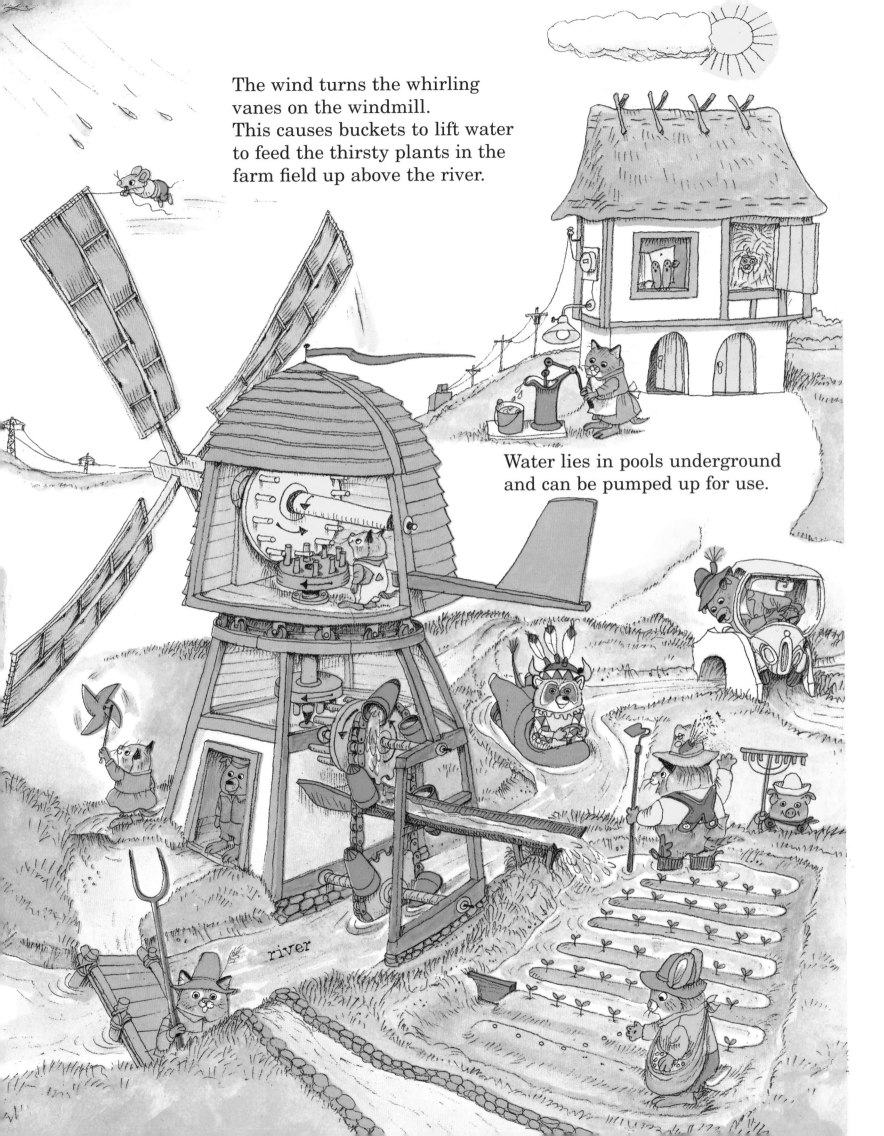

The wind turns the whirling
vanes on the windmill.
This causes buckets to lift water
to feed the thirsty plants in the
farm field up above the river.

Water lies in pools underground
and can be pumped up for use.

river

91

The river water must be made clean and pure, so that it will be safe to drink. Water is pumped into the waterworks.

The chemists put chemicals in the water to kill harmful germs.

PUMPING STATION

pump

WATERWORKS PURIFICATION PLANT

lime   alum   soda ash

CHEMICAL HOUSE

CHEMICAL SUPPLY CO.

mixing tank

PUMPING STATION

filter

sand   gravel

steam engine

chlorine kills germs

filtered water reservoir

centrifugal pump

water intake

GERMS BEWARE!

The water is clean after it flows through the waterworks.

Then the water is pumped through underground pipes to everyone.

river

riverbank

Water is used for many things. It gets dirty and must be made clean again at the sewage plant before it is put into the sea.

Water is delicious!

bathroom

hot water heater

stove

sink

kitchen

clothes washer

water hydrant

TO OTHER HOUSES

manhole cover

sewer pipe

The heat of the sun makes water return to the air. This rising water is called vapor. You cannot see water vapor, but one day it will again fall to the earth as rain or snow.

I'll see you later, water vapor!

sewage treatment plant

lighthouse

seawall

Boats use river and ocean waterways to carry people and cargo to other places.

And also— rivers and lakes and oceans are just nice to look at. Don't you think so?

This is the end of the river

You are now entering the ocean

HELP!

CLEOPATRA'S BARGE

seashore

93

Well! All the Busytown workers
have worked hard to help
their families and friends. I think it is
about time to have a party to celebrate.
Don't you?
These are the first ones to arrive
but the others are on the way.

Grocer Cat   Mommy   Huckle   Grandma   Mother Blacksmith   Junior

Daddy Pig   Mommy   Harry   Sally   Captain Salty
                                                    and some of his crew

Bugbug

bon appétit!
Dijon

Smokey   Sparky   Snozzle   Wild Bill   King Coal
                                                 Hiccup

Blacksmith Fox

Lowly Worm

HOT DOG
ROLLS

Mortimer